Thank you for everyone who helped put this book together to make it a finished product for kids to enjoy! Lizzy, Anna, Kayleigh, Mom, Dad, Hannah, Geoff, Leslie, Polly and Dominique. And a big thanks to my mentor, Link, for teaching me how to create a beautiful book. Love to all of you.
– Sarah

For Rabah who is always my support, and my two crazy cats who love doing yoga poses all day long.
– Anna

A gift for you.
Love, Sloan & Dylan xo

Dedicated to my former, current, and future Transitional Kindergarten students. And to my favorites: Cooper Graham, Cohen Samuel, Cleo Mae, Marlowe Lex, and Max George!
– Mrs. Phillips

To my wonderful daughter, Lily.
Love always, Dad.

Dear Nira, This book was written by a special friend of our family. I hope you enjoy it and have fun learning about yoga poses.
Love, Mimi.

Animal
Yoga

by
Sarah Bradshaw

illustrated by
Anna Kubaszewska

FOUR LEAF BOOKS

Good morning to you, everyone! How are you today?

I think you'll like what we have planned; we're going to stretch and play.

Animal yoga is in store; does that sound odd to you?

We'll move and tone our bodies, just like the animals do!

Yoga is an ancient art that brings us all together.

You can do it any time to help yourself feel better.

Ladybug and camel, and downward-facing dog,

Butterfly, koala, cat and jumping frog.

Are you ready? Yes, you are! First, you close your eyes.
Focus on your breathing, let thoughts just float on by.
Feel the Earth below you as you're resting on the ground.
It keeps you in the present, sitting safe and sound.

Do you feel a steady drum, deep inside your chest?

That's the beating of your heart, even while you rest.

Now make a wish, for someone else. It can be anyone.

Send your love to those who need it; now let's have some fun!

LADYBUG

Balasana

Wake up, speckled ladybug! See the morning light.

Peek out from that flower where you spent the quiet night.

Your shiny shell is brilliant red, but covered in black spots.

Do you wish that you had stripes or do you love your dots?

Fold your legs up under you, your forehead to the floor.

Curl up tight into a ball, no talking anymore.

Ladybugs aren't noisy, but they stand out in a crowd.

Furl your lovely spotted wings, shining, strong and proud.

BUTTERFLY

Baddha Konasana

Hello, butterfly! How did you sleep?

Perched on a petal, not making a peep.

Spread wide your wings and travel the sky.

Show us your colors, bright butterfly.

Take a seat and spread your knees.

Press your feet close in a squeeze.

Move your legs, first up, then down,

Like butterflies, let's float around!

DOG

Adho Mukha Svanasa

Pretty pup, come get a scratch,
Have you dug up the veggie patch?
Stand on your paws and drop your head,
Wag your tail before you're fed.

Get on all fours, hands and feet.

Then drop your head and lift your seat.

Downward dog makes your back feel good,

Stretch and bark just like a dog should!

CAT

Marjaryasana

Hello, kitty cat! What do you say?
Have you had a nap, are you ready to play?
Take a moment to lengthen your spine,
Tuck your tail under, a stretch feels fine!

Knees and hands firm on the floor,
Arch your cat back even more.
Tuck your chin and press away,
Purr like a cat, are you black, white or gray?

FROG

Malasana

"Ribbit!" says the frog, upon a lily bed.

Beside a lotus flower, pointed petals spread.

Can you use your froggy legs to jump up nice and high?

Open your mouth extra wide and catch a tasty fly.

Keep your feet a bit apart and sit low in a squat,
Bring your palms together—like that, you've hit the spot!
Hips are open side to side and spine is nice and long,
Now take a great big jump, your frog legs are so strong!

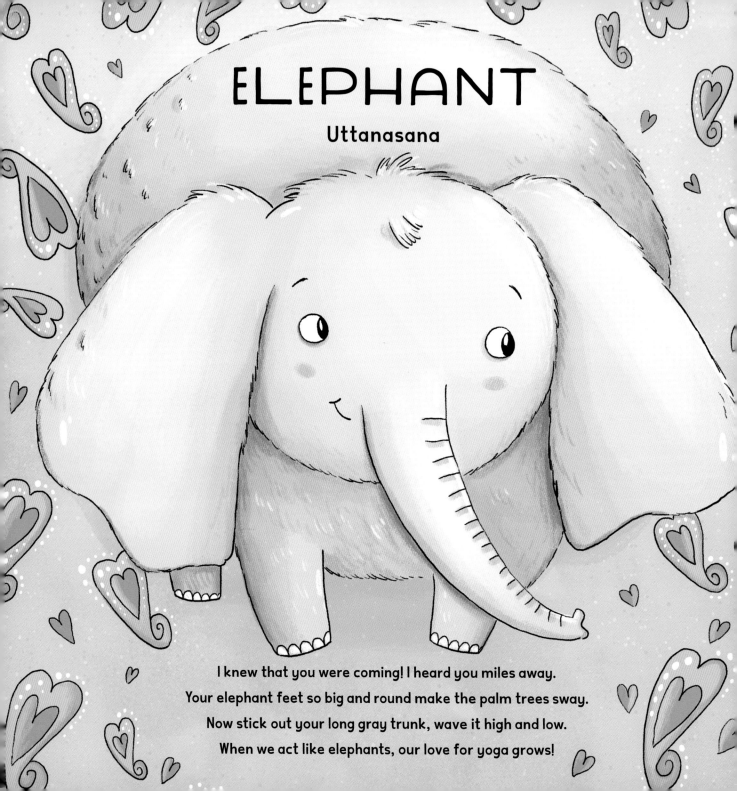

ELEPHANT

Uttanasana

I knew that you were coming! I heard you miles away.

Your elephant feet so big and round make the palm trees sway.

Now stick out your long gray trunk, wave it high and low.

When we act like elephants, our love for yoga grows!

Spread your feet apart so wide, hands come to the ground.

Lift your tail up in the air, make an elephant sound!

Bring your arms together to form a giant trunk.

Spray some water, flap your ears, take a cooling dunk.

KANGAROO

Utkatasana

Energetic kangaroo, was it a bouncy day?

Is that a joey in your pouch? Can he come out and play?

Your big feet keep you balanced, while you carry that heavy load.

Strong legs work their magic as you hop on down the road.

Bring your legs together and pretend to take a seat,

Arms out front just like a 'roo, steady on your feet.

Now the fun part can begin, bend your knees, get low.

Take a giant leap, it's an Aussie talent show!

FLAMINGO

Natarajasana

Hey there, flamingo! Standing on the shore.

Pointing downward with your beak, what are you looking for?

Your pink and fluffy feathers make me want to dance.

Twirl and spin on tippy toes, jump around and prance!

Try standing on one leg, stretch that same arm in the air,
Grab the other foot behind your back, here's a pose with flair!
Stand tall like a flamingo, long legs and graceful neck.
Reach your hand in front of you, give a friend a tiny peck!

SEAL

Bhujangasana

What's new, little seal? Basking in the sun,
Your whiskers are out and you're ready for fun!
Have you had any tasty fish today?
Shake your wet tail and get ready to play.

Roll onto your belly, give the floor a pat.

Forearms on the ground... just like that.

Pull yourself forward and flipper your feet.

Say "Arf! Arf! Arf!" — that's how seals meet!

KOALA

Garudasana

G'day, fuzzy koala, from Down Under.
You sleep for so long, it's quite a wonder.
Hugging the eucalyptus tree so tight,
To stay safely perched from morning 'til night.

Entwine your arms and give a squeeze,
Wrap your legs and bend your knees.
Challenge your balance and close your eyes,
Hug your front to your back, give it three tries!

PEACOCK
Upavistha Konasana

What magnificent feathers you have, peacock!
Can you fan them out wide and give a squawk?
The deep dark teals and golden hues,
Create some very lovely views.

To be a peacock, spread your legs wide.

Flex your feet to hold you on each side.

Reach your arms long toward your toes,

Fan your feathers and drop your nose!

GIRAFFE

Utthita Parsvakonasana

Gentle giraffe, can you hear me up there?
I see brown spots on you everywhere.
Lengthen your neck and stick out your tongue.
See the green leaves? Reach the juiciest one!

Spread your legs wide, bend your front knee.

Arms straight like the hands of a clock, don't you see?

Stretch all the way from your foot to your hand.

A giraffe grazing trees on African land.

Lie down slow and easy on your yoga mat,
Let your body be a pancake, nice and flat.
Feel the rhythm of your breath and close your eyes,
Feel the Earth below you and up above, the skies.

Take a well-earned rest right now, sink heavy to the ground.

Relax your muscles, let them go. Hear only quiet sounds.

Savasana is the final pose, the best one of them all.

Soak up that peaceful feeling, let your body sprawl.

Time to wake, come back to Earth. Open your eyes wide.

Giggle, smile and roll around. Set all your cares aside.

In Sanskrit, yoga means "unite." It links all living things.

The birds, the bees, the flowers, the trees, through winters, summers, springs.

All beings have a place on Earth, just like wise people say.

Be kind to others, and yourself. Yoga shows the way.

Namaste!

Suitable for 12 months +

ISBN 978-0-578-41963-3

Printed in 2019

Four Leaf Books
www.FourLeafBooks.com